# Contents

# rocket

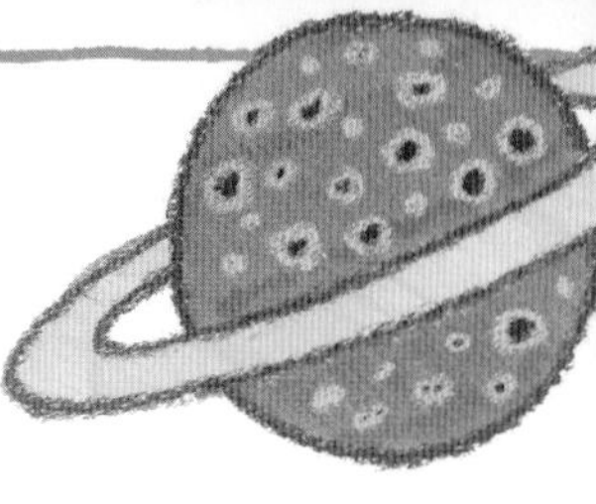

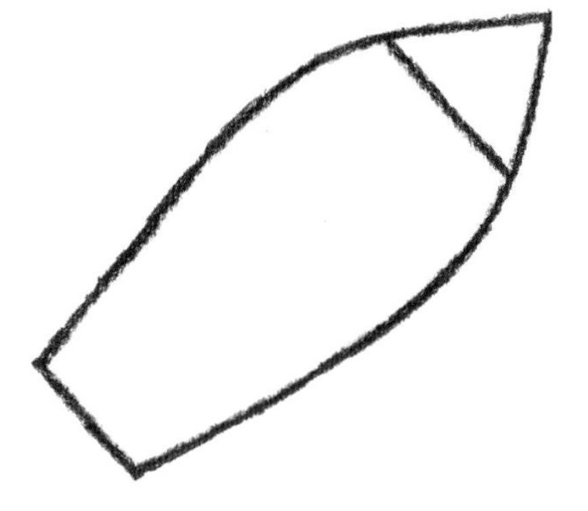

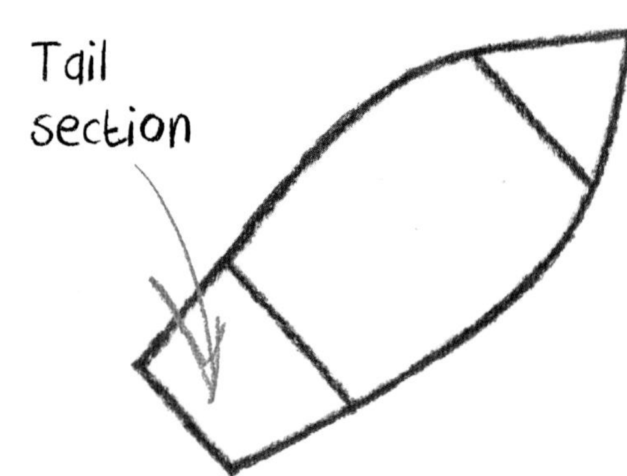


1 A rocket needs a nose cone,

2 ...a body,

3 ...a tail section,

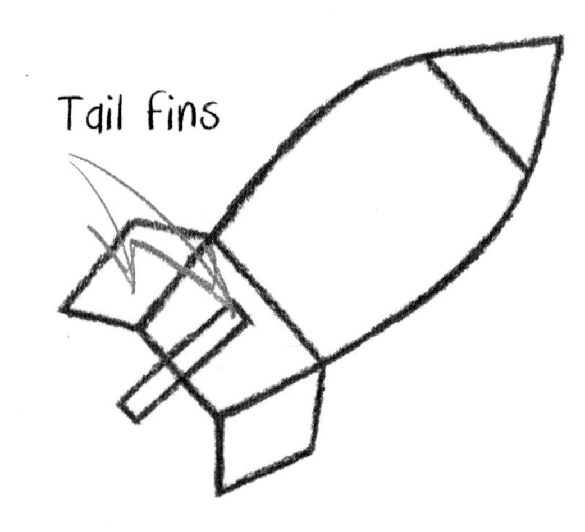

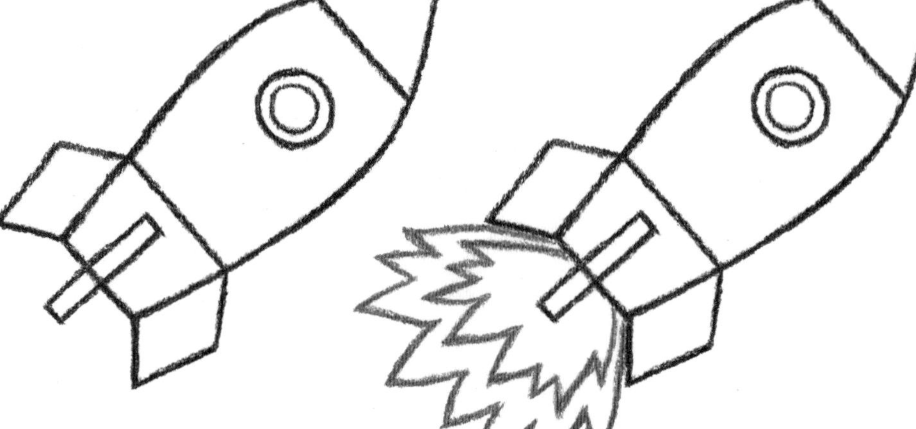

4 ...three tail fins,

5 ...and a window.

6 Now draw in some flames!

Art Work

# Drawing Things That Go

Carolyn Scrace

Author:
Carolyn Scrace graduated from Brighton College of Art, UK, with a focus on design and illustration. She has since worked in animation, advertising and children's publishing. She has a special interest in natural history and has written many books on the subject, including *Lion Journal* and *Gorilla Journal* in the *Animal Journal* series.

## How to use this book:

Follow the easy, numbered instructions. Simple step-by-step stages enable budding young artists to create their own amazing drawings.

## What you will need:

1. Paper.
2. Wax crayons.
3. Felt-tip pens to add colour.

Published in Great Britain in MMXV by
Scribblers, a division of Book House
25 Marlborough Place, Brighton BN1 1UB
**www.salariya.com**
**www.book-house.co.uk**

ISBN-13: 978-1-910184-86-8



1 3 5 7 9 8 6 4 2

A CIP catalogue record for this book is available from the British Library.

Printed and bound in China.



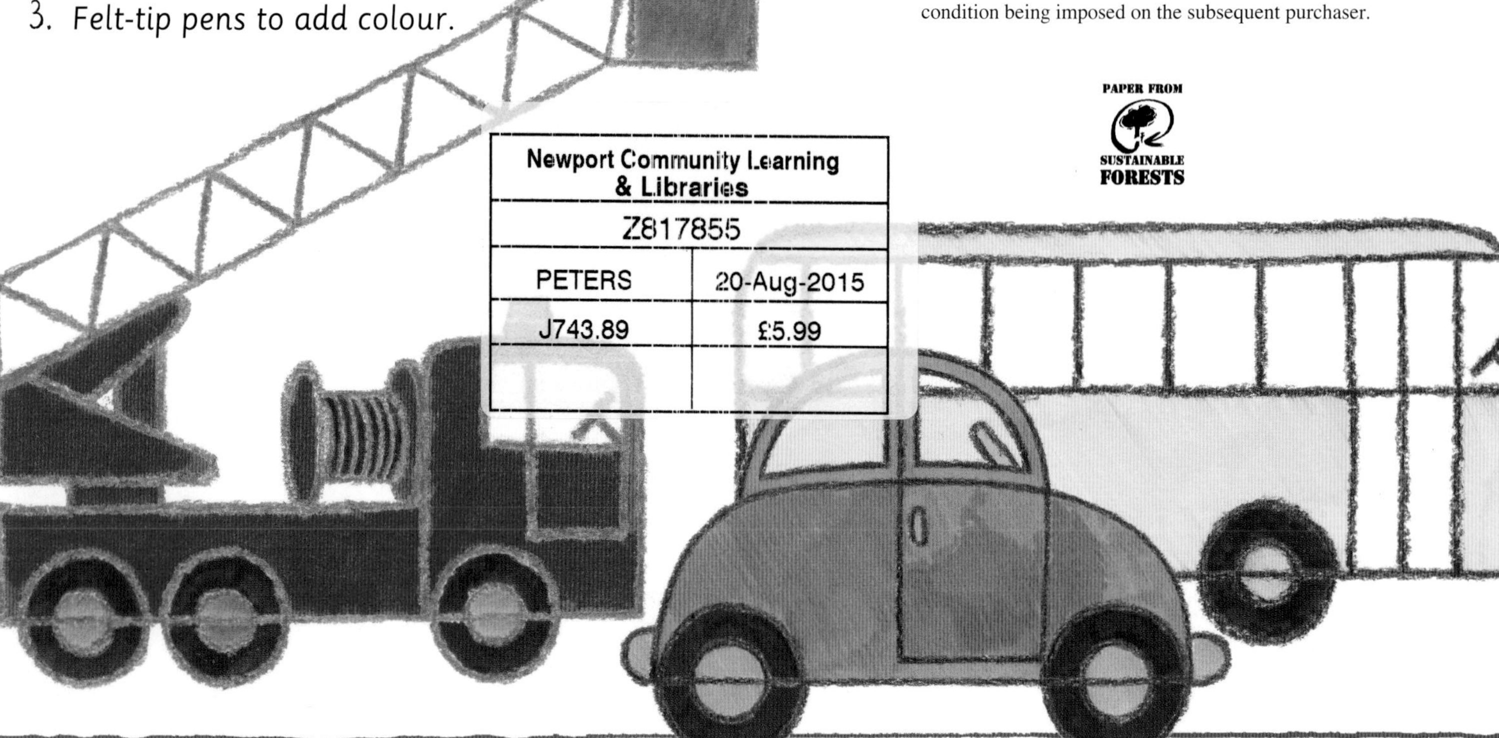

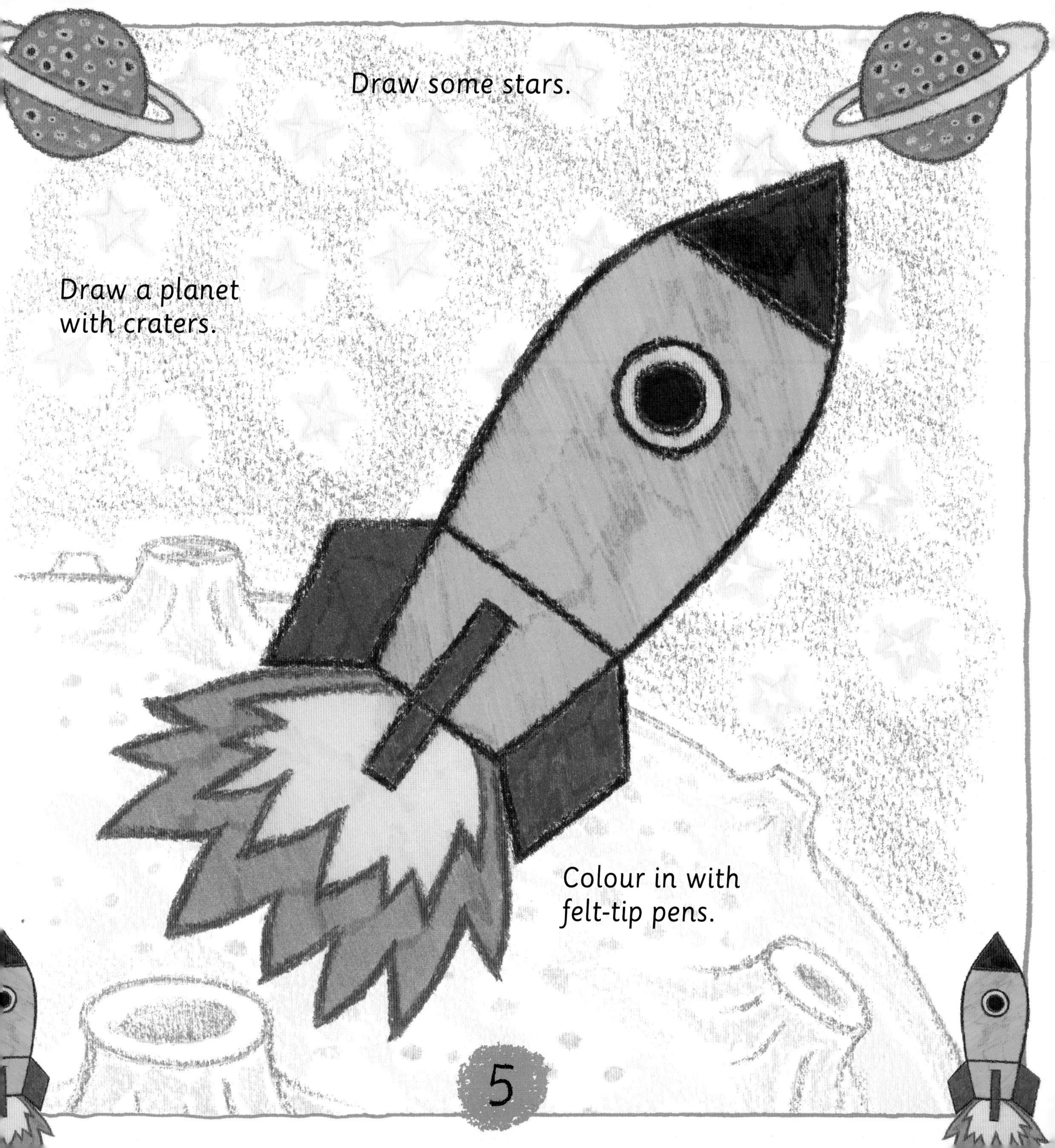
Draw some stars.
Draw a planet
with craters.
Colour in with
felt-tip pens.

# boat

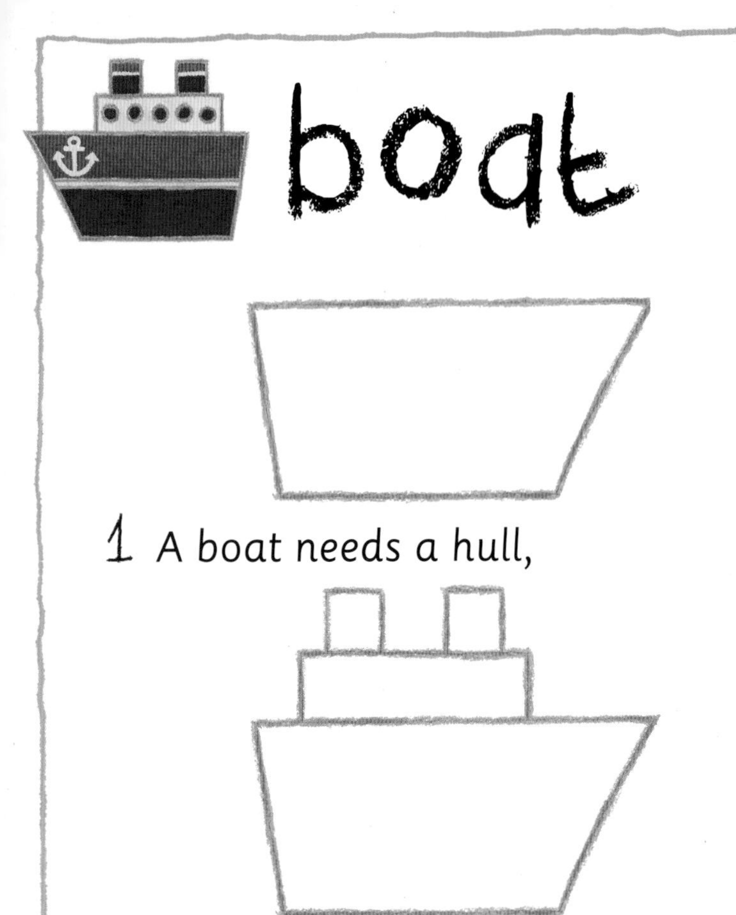

1 A boat needs a hull,

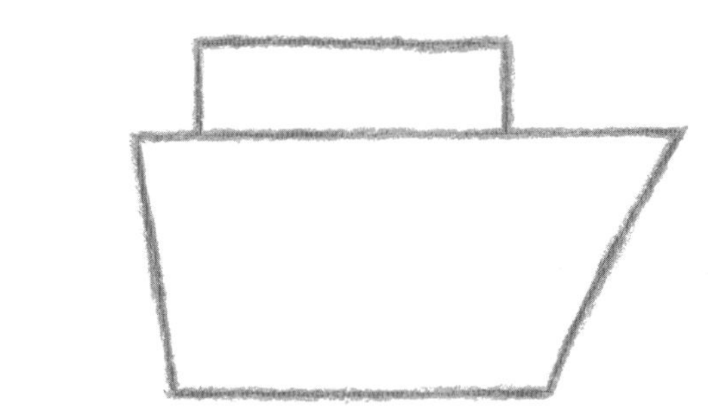

2 ...a cabin,

3 ...two funnels,

4 ...and five portholes.

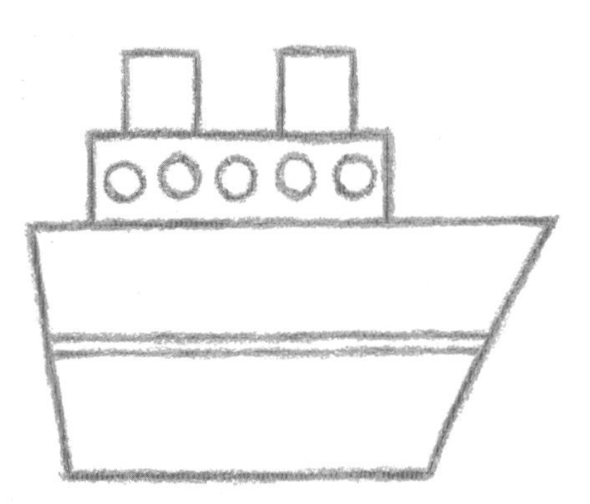

5 Draw in two stripes on the hull.

6 Then add **lots** of waves!

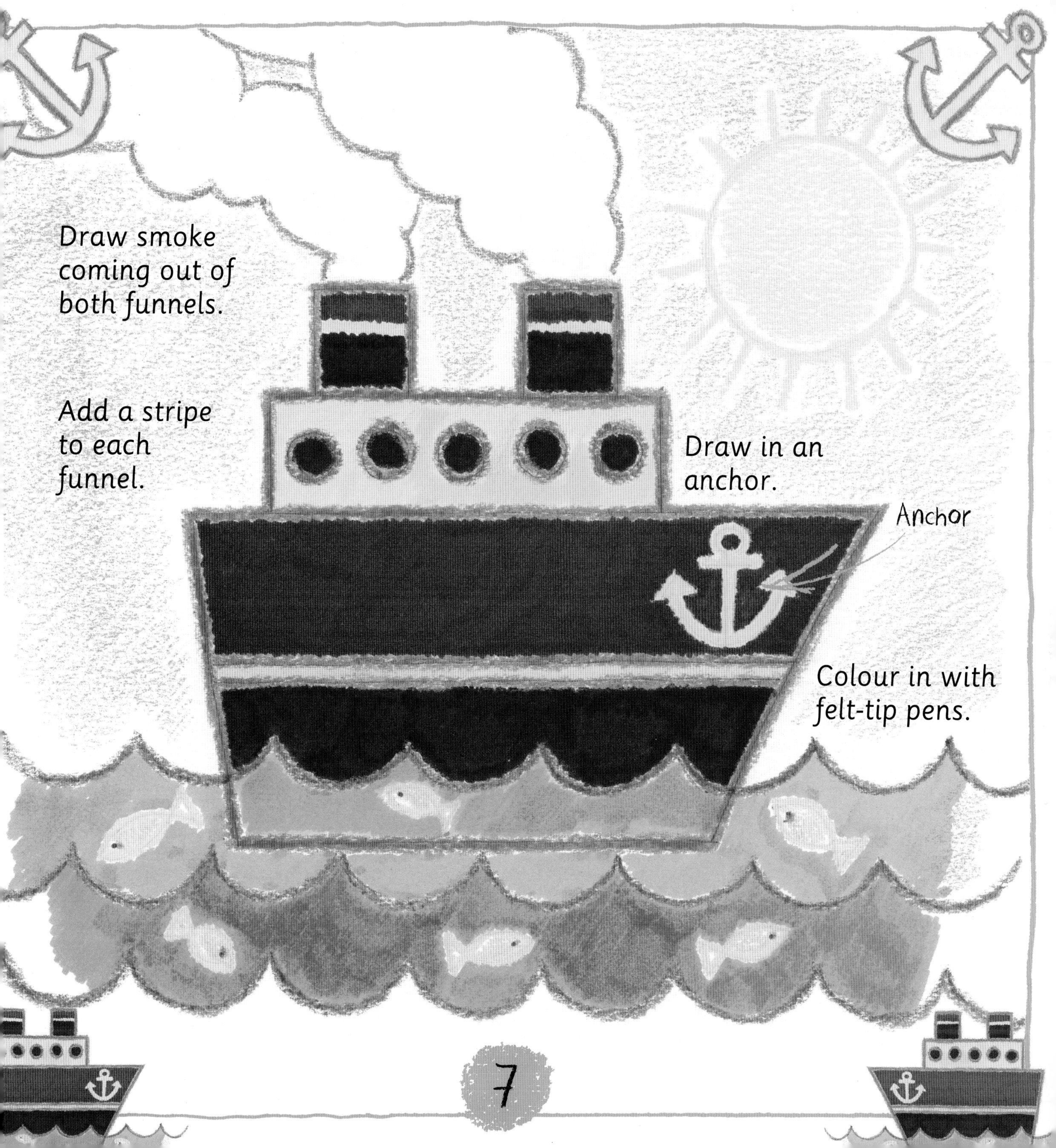
Draw smoke coming out of both funnels.
Add a stripe to each funnel.
Draw in an anchor.
Anchor
Colour in with felt-tip pens.

# aeroplane

1 An aeroplane needs a body,

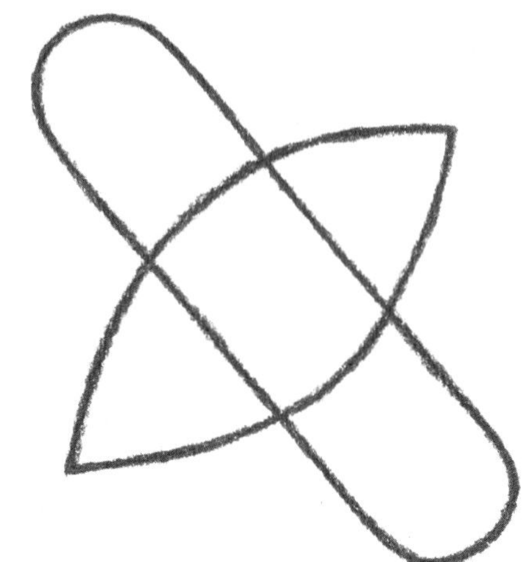

2 ...two wings,

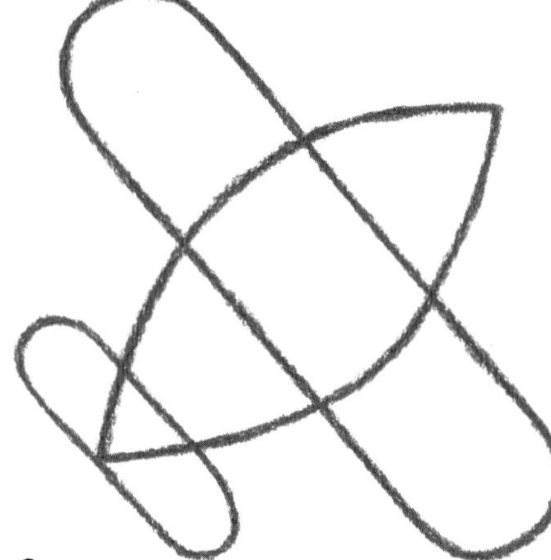

3 ...a tail,

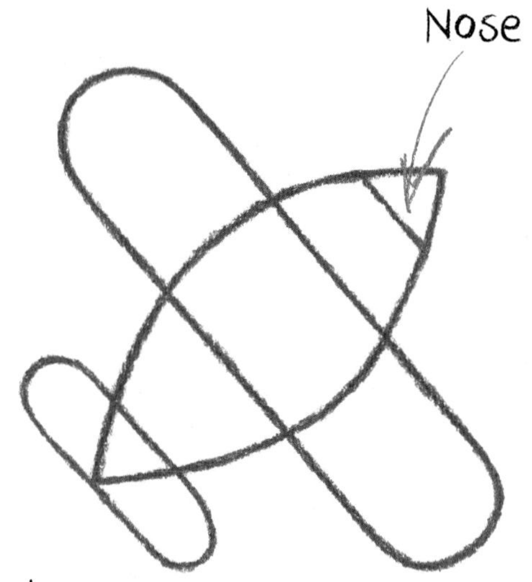


4 ...a nose section,

5 ...and a propeller.

6 Draw in the cockpit.

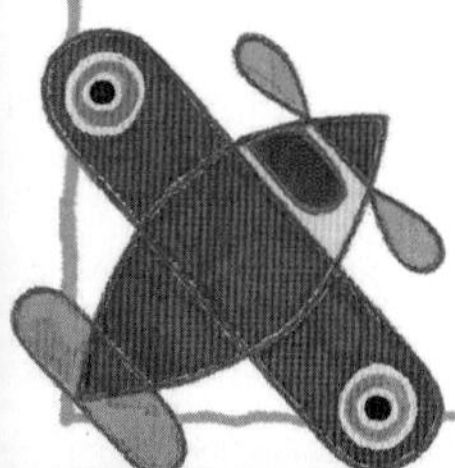

Draw circles on each wing.

Colour in with felt-tip pens.

# car

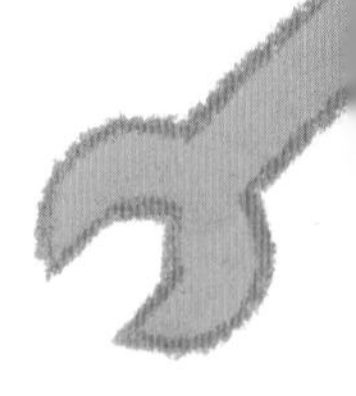

1 A car needs a body,

2 ...a roof,

3 ...two wheels,

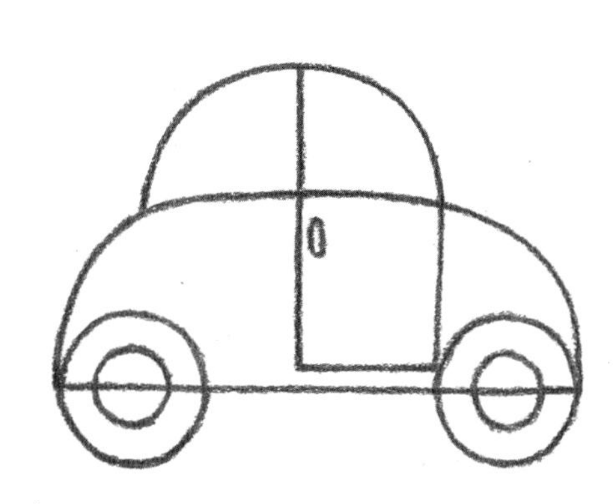

4 ...and a door and handle.

5 Draw in windows,

6 ...and two bumpers!

Now draw in the
steering wheel.
Steering
wheel
Colour in with
felt-tip pens.

# digger

1 A digger needs caterpillar tracks,

2 ...a cab,

3 ...an engine,

4 ...and a **long** arm.

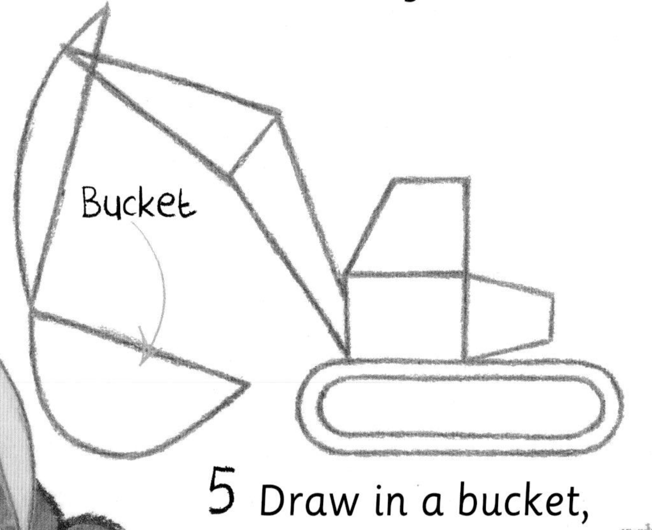


5 Draw in a bucket,

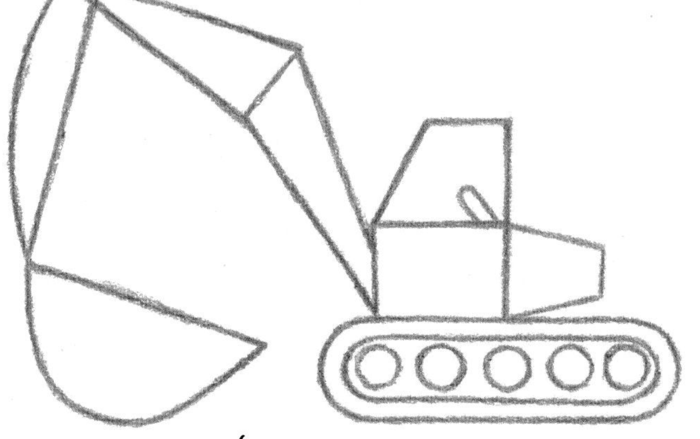

6 ...and some wheels.

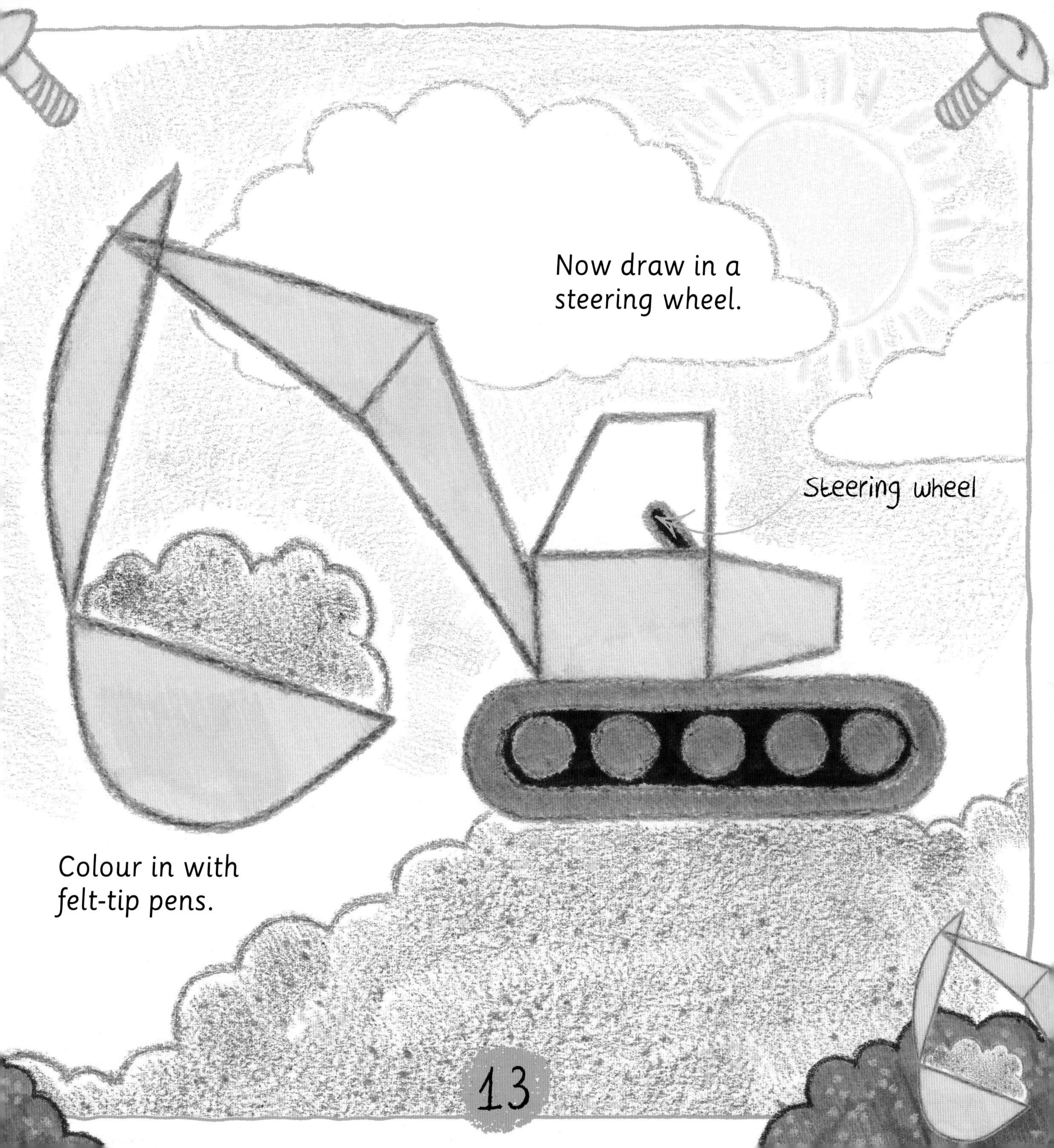
Now draw in a
steering wheel.
Steering wheel
Colour in with
felt-tip pens.

# tractor

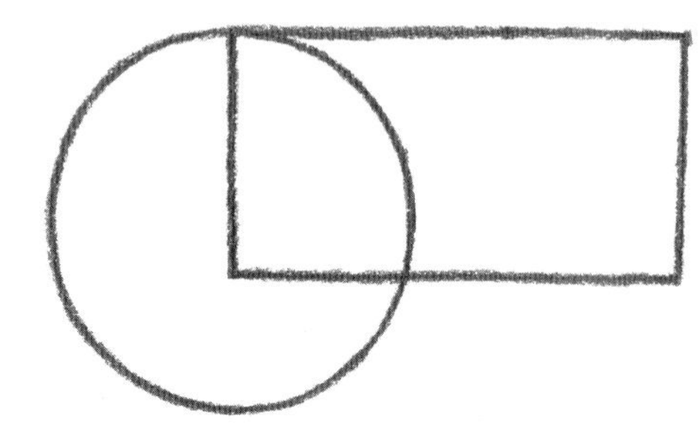

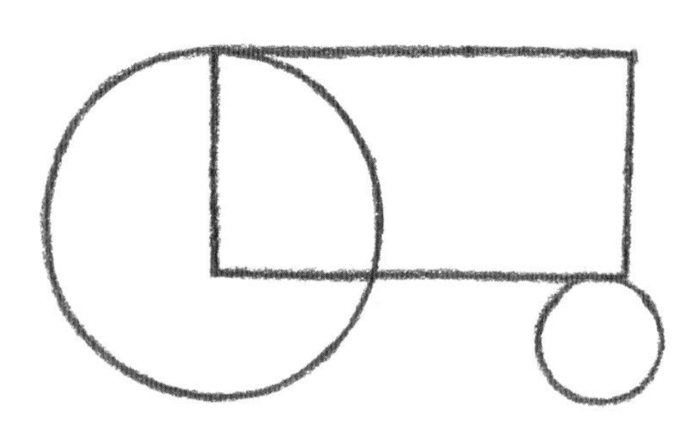

1 A tractor needs a body,

2 ...a very **big** back wheel,

3 ...a small front wheel,

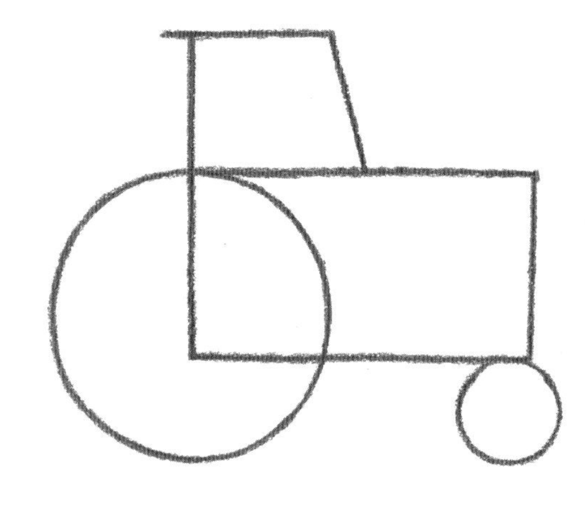

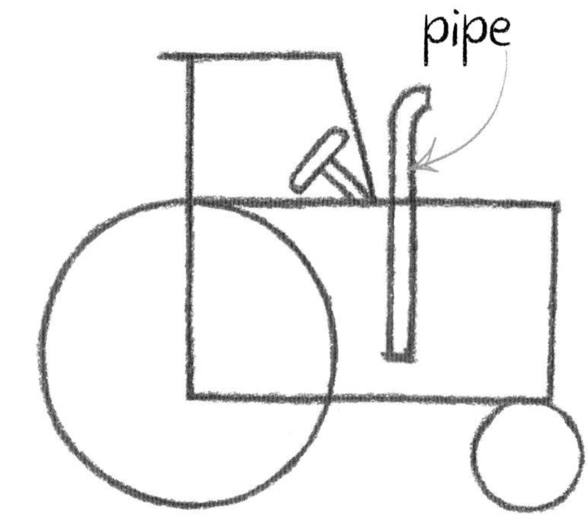


4 ...and a driver's cab.

5 Now draw in a steering wheel,

6 ...and an exhaust pipe!

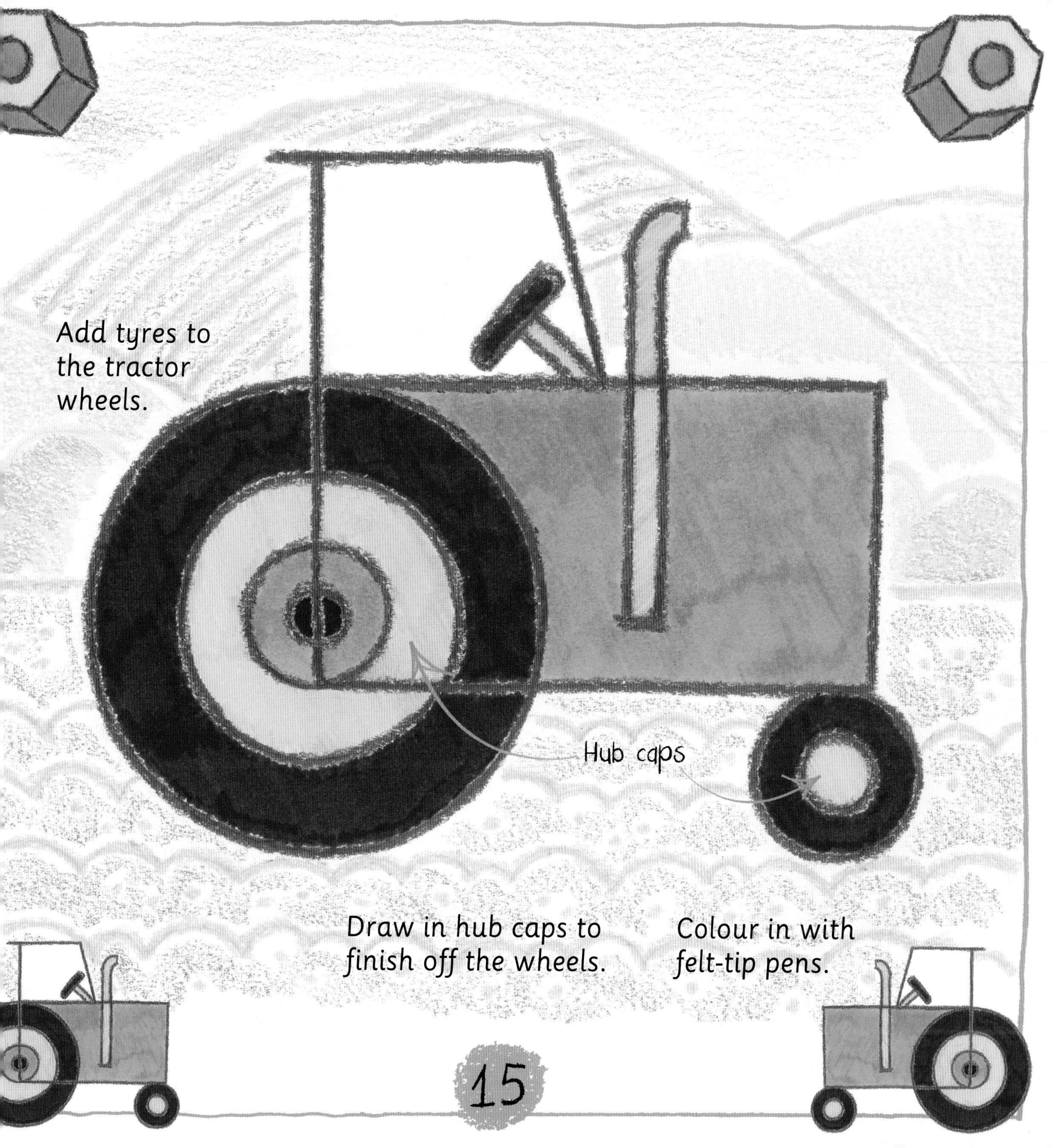


Add tyres to the tractor wheels.

Draw in hub caps to finish off the wheels.

Colour in with felt-tip pens.

# helicopter

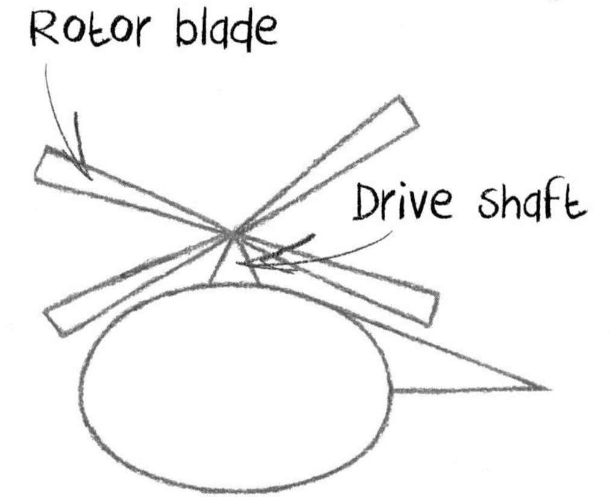


1 A helicopter needs a body,

2 ...a tail boom,

3 ...a drive shaft with **four** rotor blades,

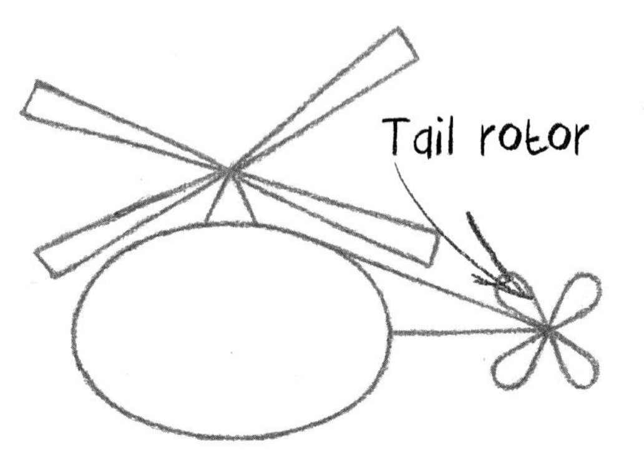


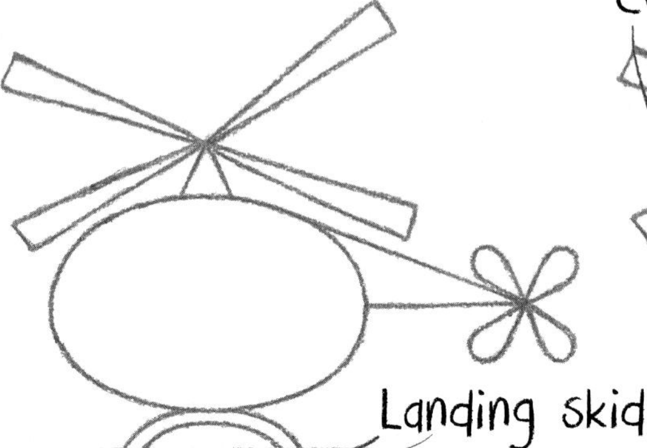


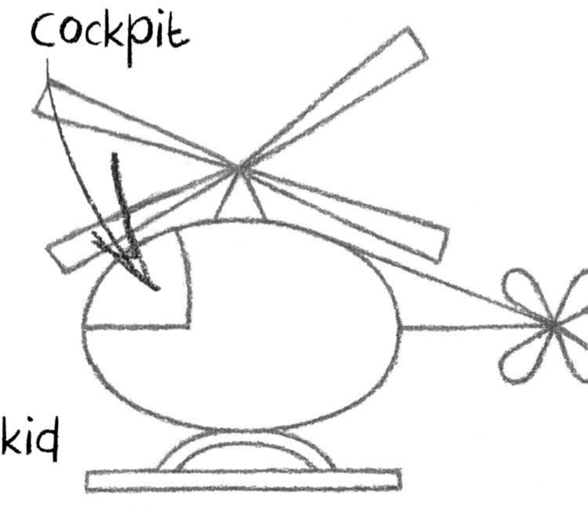


4 ...and a tail rotor!

5 Now draw in the landing skid,

6 ...and the cockpit.

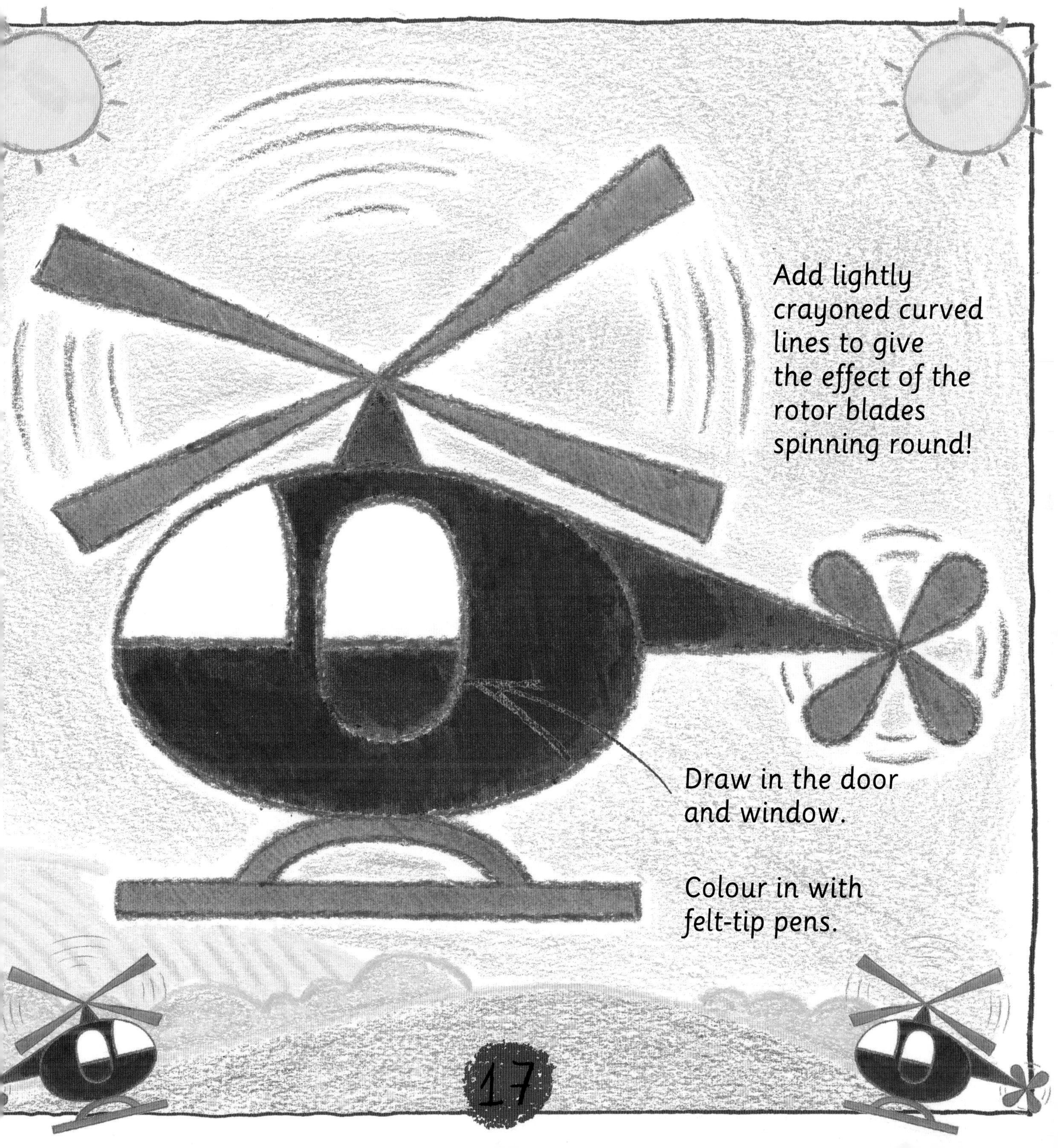
Add lightly crayoned curved lines to give the effect of the rotor blades spinning round!
Draw in the door and window.
Colour in with felt-tip pens.

# lorry

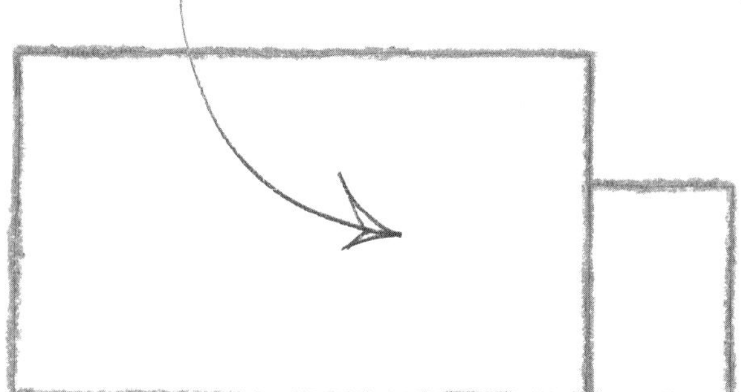

1 A lorry needs a cab,

2 ...a **big** trailer,

3 ...and three wheels.

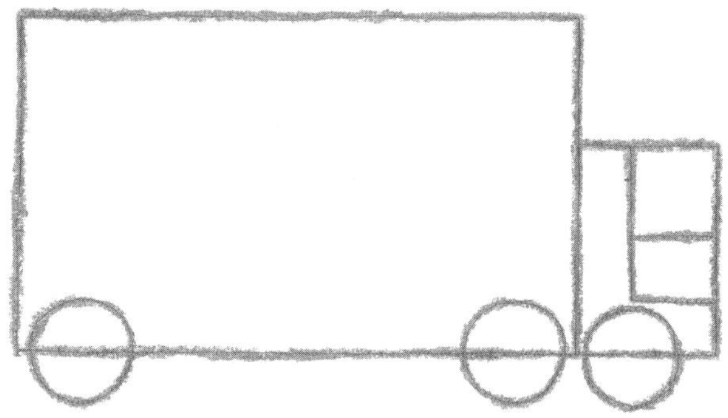

4 Draw in the cab door and window,

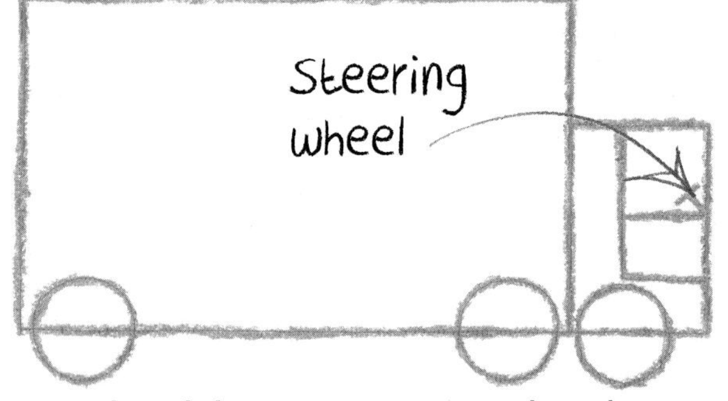


5 ...and add a steering wheel.

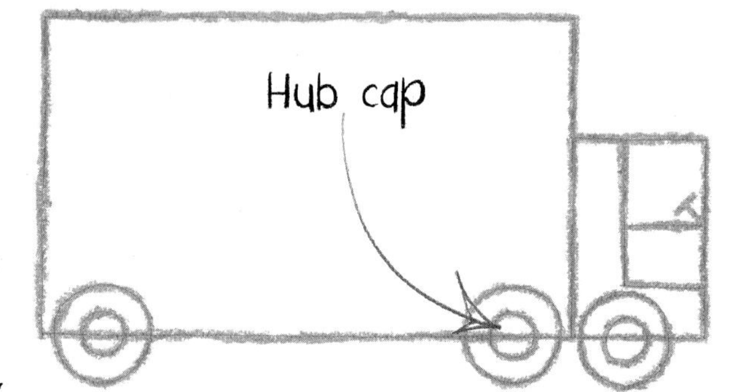


6 Draw in the hub caps.

Draw in a
door handle.
Door
handle
Colour in with
felt-tip pens.

# fire engine

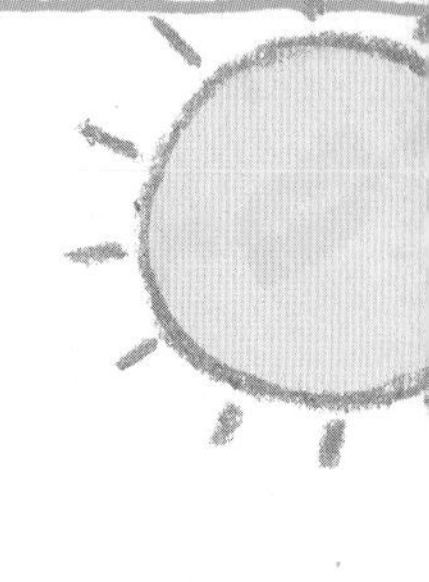

1 A fire engine needs a cab,

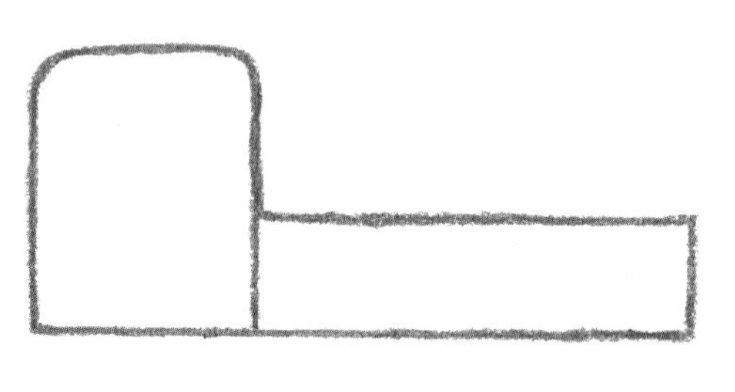

2 ...a long rear section,

3 ...and three wheels.

4 Draw in the cab door and windows.

5 Add a lifting device at the back,

6 ...with a **long** arm and cradle.

Finish off the arm
with a crayoned
zigzag line.
Draw in the
light and the
steering wheel.
Draw in the
reel and hose.
Add hub caps.
Colour in with
felt-tip pens.

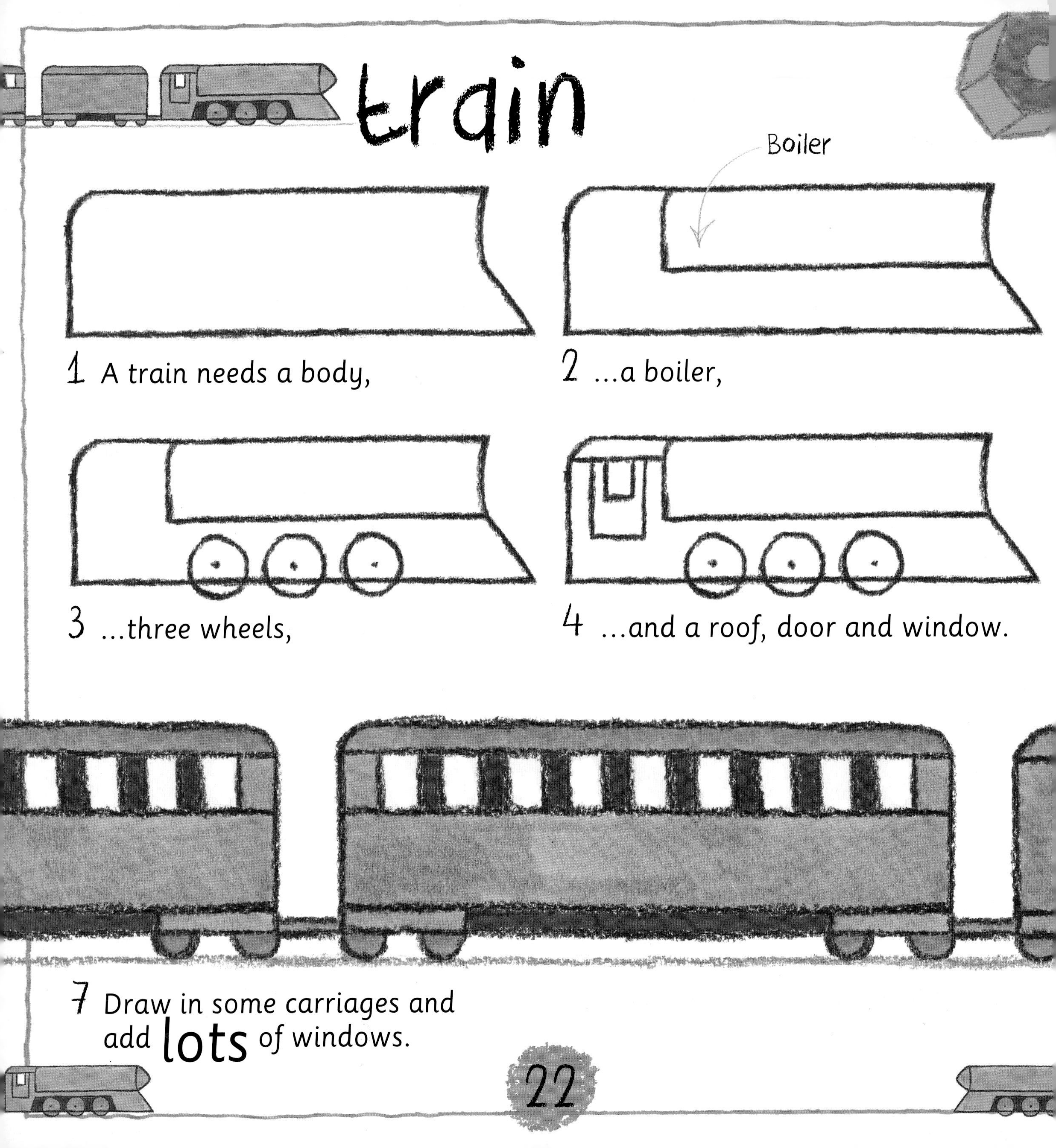
train
Boiler
1 A train needs a body,
2 ...a boiler,
3 ...three wheels,
4 ...and a roof, door and window.
7 Draw in some carriages and
add lots of windows.

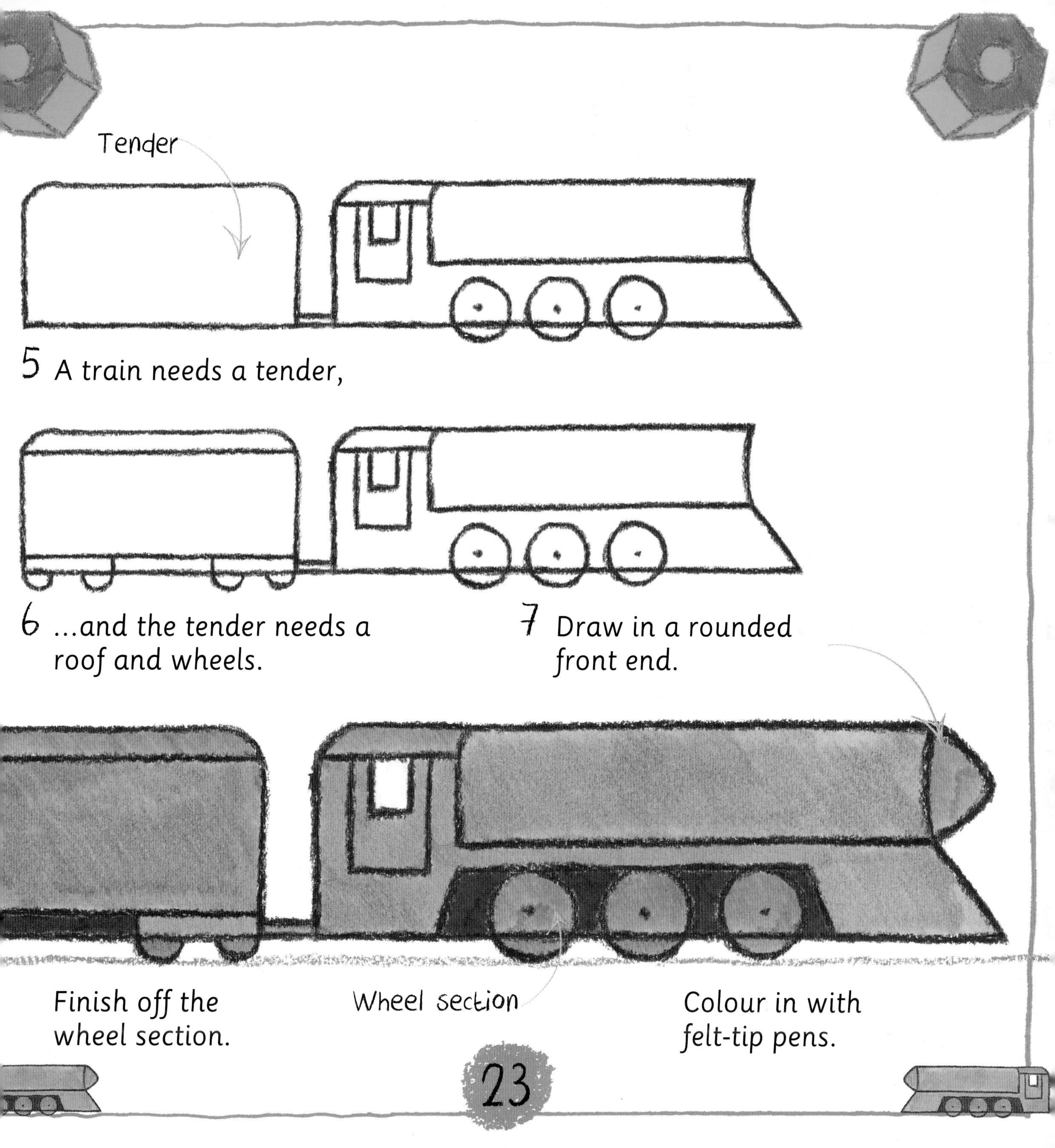


5 A train needs a tender,

6 ...and the tender needs a roof and wheels.

7 Draw in a rounded front end.

Finish off the wheel section.

Colour in with felt-tip pens.

# bus

1 A bus needs a body,

2 ...a roof,

3 ...a side panel,

4 ...and doors.

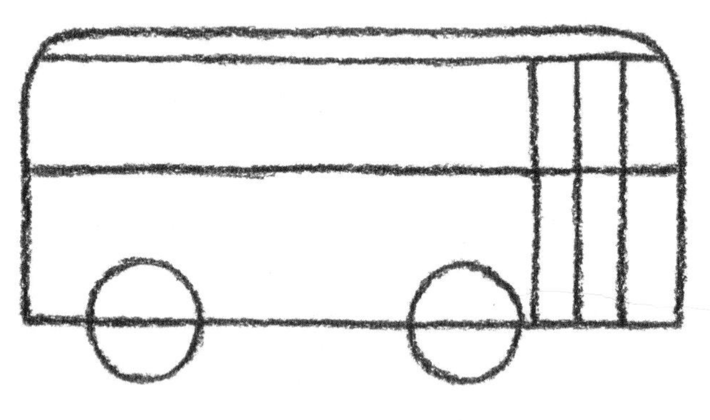

5 Now draw in two wheels,

6 ...and **lots** of windows!

Draw in a
steering wheel.
Add the
hub caps.
Colour in with
felt-tip pens.

# snow plough

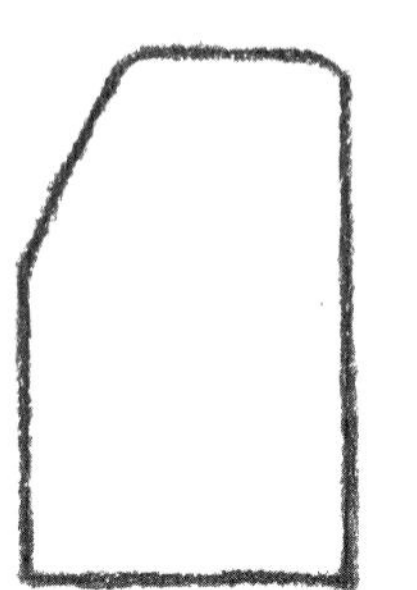

1 A snow plough needs a cab,

2 ...a body,

3 ...and three wheels.

Plough blade

4 Draw in the plough blade.

5 Add a door and windows.

6 ...and a line for the salt carrier.

Draw in a
flashing light!
Add a steering wheel.
Crayon in
hub caps.
Colour in with
felt-tip pens.

# bicycle

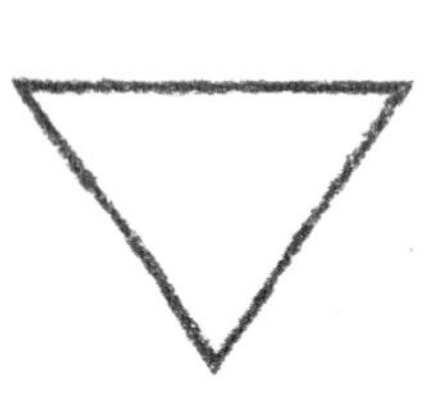

1 A bicycle needs a frame,

2 ...two wheels,

3 ...a front fork with handlebars,

4 ...and a back fork and a saddle.

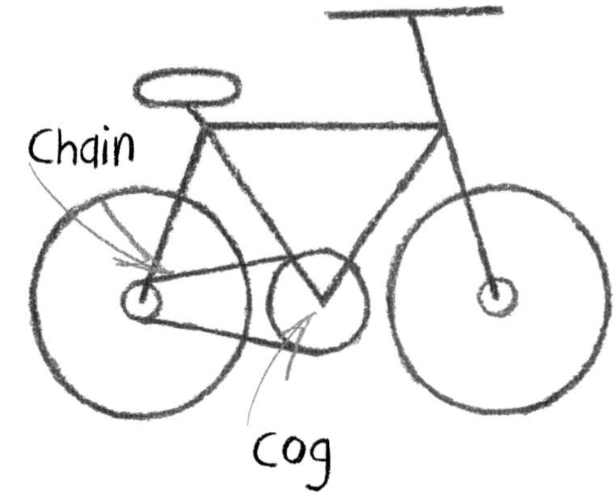


5 Draw in a round cog, and a chain,

6 ...and two pedals.

Draw in the tyres and lots of spokes.

Colour in with felt-tip pens.

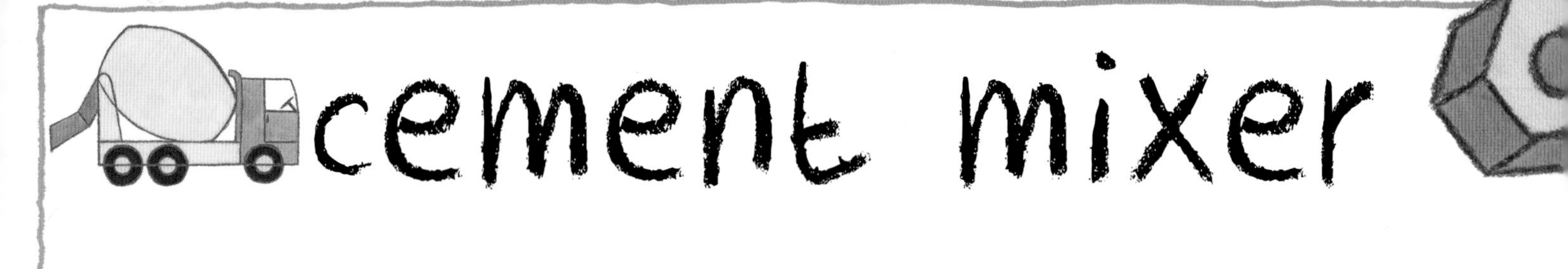

# cement mixer

1 A cement mixer lorry needs a cab,

2 ...a tail section,

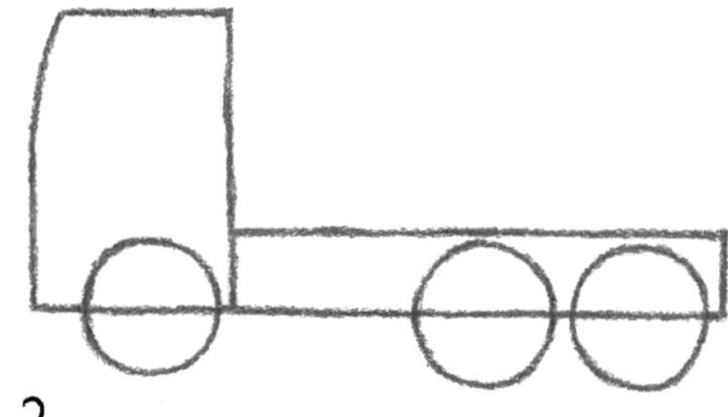

3 ...and three wheels.

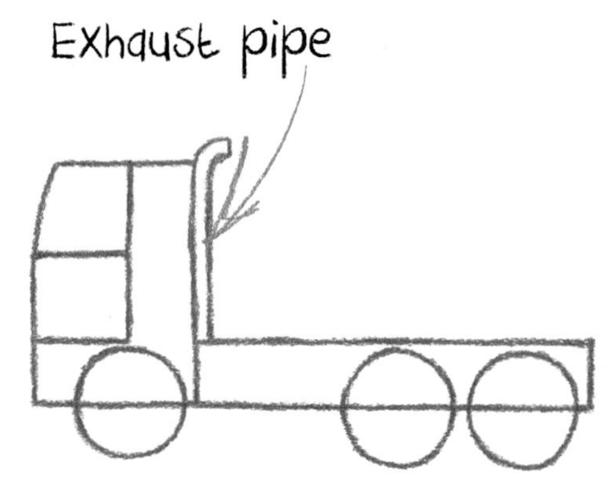



4 Draw in the cab door and window. Add an exhaust pipe!

5 Now draw in a **big** mixing drum,

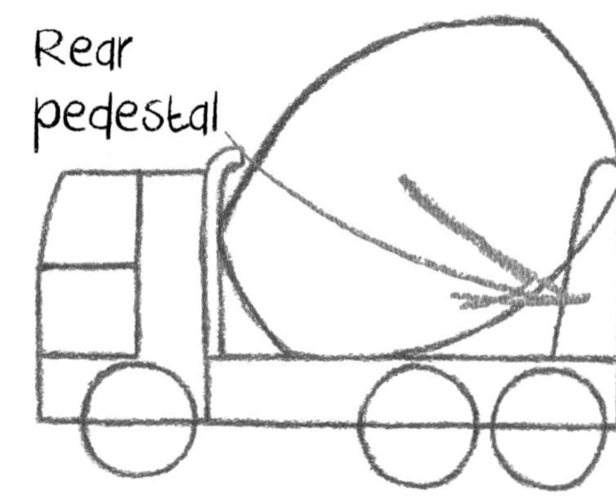



6 ...and a rear pedestal.

Draw in
the chute.
Add the
steering wheel.
Chute
Draw in hub caps.
Colour in with
felt-tip pens.

# glossary

**Boiler** the part of a steam engine where water is boiled to make steam.

**Caterpillar track** a track made of metal or rubber plates joined together. Vehicles with these tracks can go over rough ground easily.

**Cockpit** the part of an aeroplane where the pilot sits.

**Exhaust pipe** the part of a vehicle where the exhaust smoke comes out.

**Rotor blades** the big propeller on the top of a helicopter which makes it go up and down.

**Tail fins** the short wings at the back of a rocket or aeroplane.

**Tender** a truck carrying coal and water that goes behind a steam engine.

# index